YOU'RE MY BOO

Kate Dopirak   Lesley Breen Withrow

Beach Lane Books • New York London Toronto Sydney New Delhi

You're my peek-a-boo,
my sneak-a-boo,

my laughing-till-you-squeak-a-boo.

Go!   Stop!

Walk!   Run!

You're my funny honey bun.

You're my race-a-boo,
my chase-a-boo,
my flying-into-space-a-boo.

Laugh!   Cry!

Build!   Break!

You're my pumpkin doodle cake.

You're my glide-a-boo,
my slide-a-boo,
my want-to-take-a-ride-a-boo.

Yes!   No!

Nice!   Mean!

You're my stinky jelly bean.

You're my yuck-a-boo,
my yum-a-boo,
my banging-like-a-drum-a-boo.

Yikes!   Yay!

Climb!   Fall!

You're my goofy bouncy ball.

You're my mess-a-boo,
undressed-a-boo,
my bubbles-are-the-BEST-a-boo.

Cool!   Warm!

Wet!   Dry!

You're my quiet dragonfly.

You're my bug-a-boo,
my hug-a-boo,

my sleepy, cozy snug-a-boo.

And no matter *what* you do . . .

you will *always* be my boo.

For my pumpkin doodle cakes:
Josh, Joey, Bobby, and Frankie
–K. D.

For my sister, Sandy–my best friend growing up–
and for Mom, Steven, and Marin, with much love
–L. B. W.

BEACH LANE BOOKS • An imprint of Simon & Schuster Children's Publishing Division • 1230 Avenue of the Americas, New York, New York 10020 • Text copyright © 2016 by Kate Dopirak • Illustrations copyright © 2016 by Lesley Breen Withrow • All rights reserved, including the right of reproduction in whole or in part in any form. • BEACH LANE BOOKS is a trademark of Simon & Schuster, Inc. • For information about special discounts for bulk purchases, please contact Simon & Schuster Special Sales at 1-866-506-1949 or business@simonandschuster.com. • The Simon & Schuster Speakers Bureau can bring authors to your live event. For more information or to book an event, contact the Simon & Schuster Speakers Bureau at 1-866-248-3049 or visit our website at www.simonspeakers.com. • Book design by Lauren Rille • The text for this book was set in Caitiff. • The illustrations for this book were rendered in pencil and colored with hand-painted collage pieces and digital painting. • Manufactured in China • 0716 SCP • First Edition • 10 9 8 7 6 5 4 3 2 1 • Library of Congress Cataloging-in-Publication Data • Names: Dopirak, Kate, author. | Withrow, Lesley Breen, illustrator. • Title: You're my boo / Kate Dopirak ; illustrated by Lesley Breen Withrow. • Other titles: You are my boo • Description: First edition. | New York : Beach Lane Books, [2016] | Summary: "A sweet, rhyming ode to unconditional love and the ups and downs of family life"—Provided by publisher. • Identifiers: LCCN 2015033747 | ISBN 9781442441606 (hardcover) | ISBN 9781442441613 (eBook) • Subjects: | CYAC: Love—Fiction. | Family life—Fiction. | Stories in rhyme. • Classification: LCC PZ8.3.D7334 Yo 2016 | DDC [E]—dc23 LC record available at http://lccn.loc.gov/2015033747